Still Waiting

To polar bears,
And to all the children
who want to make a difference for them

by Danielle Lee

This is Ollie. Ollie is a polar bear cub, which is a baby polar bear. Ollie lives at the tippy top of the globe, in a place called the Arctic Circle. It is very cold and snowy up there, but Ollie is warm because of his thick fur and blubber.

Este es Ollie. Ollie es un cachorro de oso polar, que es un oso polar bebé. Ollie vive en la cima del globo terráqueo, en un lugar llamado Círculo Polar Ártico. Hace mucho frío y nieva allí arriba, pero Ollie está caliente debido a su espeso pelaje y grasa.

This is Ollie's mother. Ollie's mother loves Ollie very much. When Ollie was very little, she fed him her milk because he could not eat solid food yet. And when Ollie got older, she caught him seals, which is his favorite food.

Esta es la madre de Ollie. La madre de Ollie quiere mucho a Ollie. Cuando Ollie era muy pequeño, ella lo alimentaba con leche porque aún no podía comer alimentos sólidos. Y cuando Ollie creció, le atrapó focas, que es su comida favorita.

While Ollie's mother was out hunting for seals, Ollie stayed home and watched TV. He was still too young to go outside by himself.

Mientras la madre de Ollie salió a cazar focas, Ollie se quedó en casa y vio la televisión. Todavía era demasiado joven para salir solo.

Once, there was a pigeon reporting for a news channel on TV. The pigeon was in New York City! She talked about pollution and global warming, but Ollie did not really understand what she was talking about.

Una vez, había una paloma informando para un canal de noticias en la televisión. ¡La paloma estaba en la ciudad de Nueva York! Habló sobre la contaminación y el calentamiento global, pero Ollie no entendía realmente de qué estaba hablando.

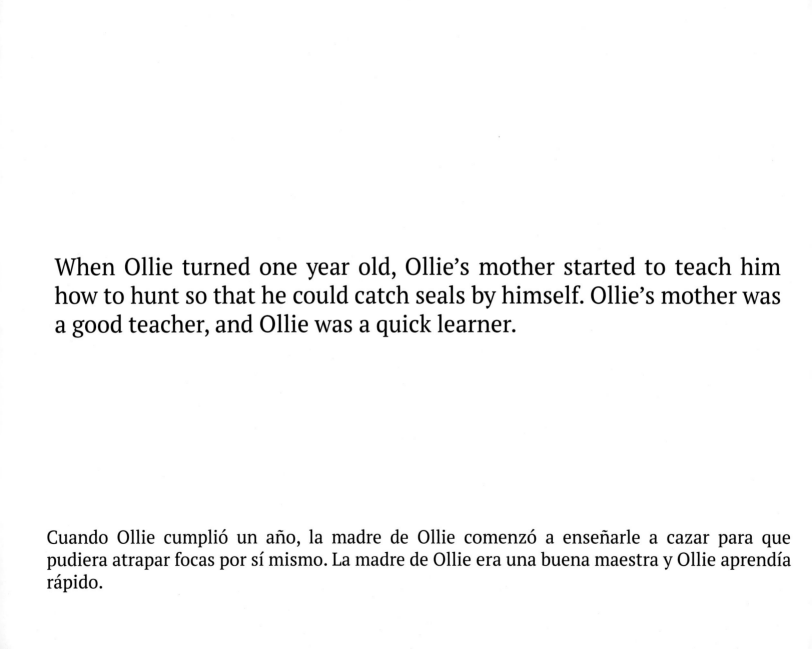

When Ollie turned one year old, Ollie's mother started to teach him how to hunt so that he could catch seals by himself. Ollie's mother was a good teacher, and Ollie was a quick learner.

Cuando Ollie cumplió un año, la madre de Ollie comenzó a enseñarle a cazar para que pudiera atrapar focas por sí mismo. La madre de Ollie era una buena maestra y Ollie aprendía rápido.

Here is a picture of Ollie with his first seal!

¡Aquí hay una foto de Ollie con su primer foca!

But then, ice in the Arctic started to melt. Ollie's mother told him that it was too dangerous for him to hunt on his own anymore. Ollie thought this was very unfair, since he had only just begun catching his own food.

Pero luego, el hielo en el Ártico comenzó a derretirse. La madre de Ollie le dijo que ya era demasiado peligroso para él cazar solo. Ollie pensó que esto era muy injusto, ya que apenas había comenzado a pescar su propia comida.

But over time, Ollie understood why his mother was being so strict. Polar bears cannot swim for long underwater, so they use ice as a resting place while they hunt. But if that ice disappears, polar bears no longer have a place to rest. So if they run out of energy mid-hunt, they could end up drowning or returning home without any food.

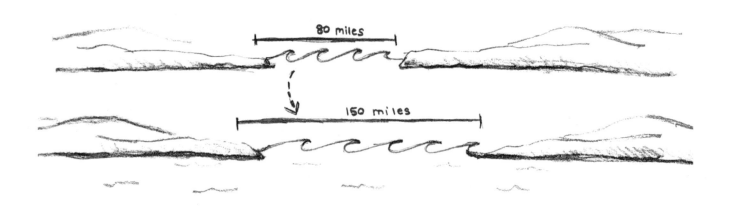

Pero con el tiempo, Ollie comprendió por qué su madre era tan estricta. Los osos polares no pueden nadar mucho tiempo bajo el agua, por lo tanto utilizan el hielo como lugar de descanso mientras cazan. Pero si ese hielo desaparece, los osos polares ya no tendrán un lugar para descansar. Entonces, si se quedan sin energía a mitad de la caza, podrían terminar ahogándose o regresando a casa sin comida.

Seals were especially hard to catch, since they lived deep in the sea. So instead, Ollie's mother came home with small bird eggs or fish, but that was not enough food for Ollie and his mother.

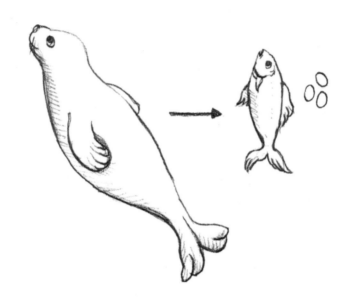

Las focas eran especialmente difíciles de atrapar, ya que vivían en las profundidades del mar. Entonces, en cambio, la madre de Ollie llegó a casa con huevos de pájaros pequeños o peces, pero eso no fue suficiente comida para Ollie y su madre.

One day, Ollie's mother looked at Ollie and saw how hungry he was. Ollie's mother loved her cub very much, and she was sad to see him suffer.

"I promise to bring back a seal this time," she said.

Un día, la madre de Ollie miró a Ollie y vio lo hambriento que estaba el. La madre de Ollie quería mucho a su cachorro y estaba triste de verlo sufrir.

"Prometo traer de vuelta una foca esta vez", dijo la mama.

As Ollie's mother went out to hunt for a seal, Ollie turned on the TV to watch the news again. This time, there was a dog reporting from Paris.

Cuando la madre de Ollie salió a buscar una foca, Ollie encendió la televisión para volver a ver las noticias. Esta vez, había un perro informando desde París.

"Global warming happens when cars or factories produce gas," the dog said. "These gases are very harmful to the earth. They trap heat in the air, which raises the earth's temperature."

"El calentamiento global ocurre cuando los automóviles o las fábricas producen gas", dijo el perro. "Estos gases son muy dañinos para la tierra. Atrapan el calor en el aire, y elevan la temperatura de la tierra ".

Ollie wanted to share what he learned with his mother. Could global warming be the cause of the ice melting?

Ollie quería compartir lo que aprendió con su madre. ¿Podría el calentamiento global ser la causa del derretimiento del hielo?

"Mom!" Ollie yelled. He looked around on the ice, but he did not see her. "Mom! I have something to tell you!"

"¡Mamá!" Ollie gritó. Miró alrededor en el hielo, pero no la vio. "¡Mamá! ¡Tengo algo que contarte!"

Ollie searched for his mother everywhere, but the ice and sea around him were lifeless. He ran back home, thinking maybe she had already came back. But the house was empty, too.

Ollie buscó a su madre por todas partes, pero el hielo y el mar a su alrededor estaban sin vida. Corrió de regreso a casa, pensando que tal vez ella ya había regresado. Pero la casa también estaba vacía.

Ollie sat at the front door, waiting for his mother to come home. But the sun set, and still she did not come.

Ollie se sentó en la puerta principal, esperando que su madre volviera a casa. Pero el sol se puso y ella seguía sin venir.

(Draw your own sunset!)

(¡Dibuja tu propia puesta de sol!)

Author's Note

What is global warming?

➜ When fossil fuels such as coal, gas, and oil are burned, harmful gases called greenhouse gases are released into the earth's atmosphere. Those gases trap heat from the sun, which causes an increase in the earth's global temperature.

Why are polar bears so heavily affected by global warming?

➜ The rise of global temperatures causes sea ice to melt, which destroys the polar bears' habitats. Ice is essential for food, home, and resting areas while hunting.

➜ With the ice surface decreasing, polar bears have been struggling to catch their main source of food (seals), because they cannot swim for a long period of time without rest. Some polar bears have been eating eggs or fish recently, which lack the necessary nutrients they need.

How to Help

Save energy!

Ways to save energy:
- → Turn off the sink water when you're not using it
- → Recycle and try to avoid using plastic (ex: plastic straws, plastic bags)
- → Walk/bike instead of taking the car if it's safe
- → Plant trees or any other plants! They help get rid of harmful gases
- → Turn off any electronics (TV, computer, lights) when you're not using them

Keep learning!

Keep reading and learning more about global warming to educate yourself!

Share with others!

Share with your friends or family about what you learned and how they can help! The more the better :)

Essential thanks to Julie Bahn for help with illustrations and Spanish translations.

About the Author & Illustrator

Danielle Lee is a student at Biotechnology High School in New Jersey, USA. She is passionate about environmental and animal rights, writing, and science research.